Dear Parent:
Your child's love of reading starts here!

Every child learns to read in a different way and at his or her own speed. Some go back and forth between reading levels and read favorite books again and again. Others read through each level in order. You can help your young reader improve and become more confident by encouraging his or her own interests and abilities. From books your child reads with you to the first books he or she reads alone, there are I Can Read Books for every stage of reading:

SHARED READING
Basic language, word repetition, and whimsical illustrations, ideal for sharing with your emergent reader

BEGINNING READING
Short sentences, familiar words, and simple concepts for children eager to read on their own

READING WITH HELP
Engaging stories, longer sentences, and language play for developing readers

READING ALONE
Complex plots, challenging vocabulary, and high-interest topics for the independent reader

ADVANCED READING
Short paragraphs, chapters, and exciting themes for the perfect bridge to chapter books

I Can Read Books have introduced children to the joy of reading since 1957. Featuring award-winning authors and illustrators and a fabulous cast of beloved characters, I Can Read Books set the standard for beginning readers.

A lifetime of discovery begins with the magical words **"I Can Read!"**

Visit www.icanread.com for information
on enriching your child's reading experience.

Pinkalicious®
and the Perfect Present

To Mom

—V.K.

The author gratefully acknowledges
the artistic and editorial contributions of
Robert Masheris and Gabrielle Balkan.

I Can Read Book® is a trademark of HarperCollins Publishers.

Pinkalicious and the Perfect Present
Copyright © 2014 by Victoria Kann

PINKALICIOUS and all related logos and characters are trademarks of Victoria Kann. Used with permission.

Based on the HarperCollins book *Pinkalicious* written by
Victoria Kann and Elizabeth Kann, illustrated by Victoria Kann
All rights reserved. Manufactured in China.
No part of this book may be used or reproduced in any manner whatsoever without
written permission except in the case of brief quotations embodied in critical articles and reviews.
For information address HarperCollins Children's Books, a division of HarperCollins Publishers,
10 East 53rd Street, New York, NY 10022.
www.icanread.com

Library of Congress catalog card number: 2013936298

ISBN 978-0-06-218789-5 (trade bdg.)—ISBN 978-0-06-218788-8 (pbk.)

13 14 15 16 17   SCP   10 9 8 7 6 5 4 3 2 1
❖
First Edition

I Can Read!

BEGINNING 1 READING

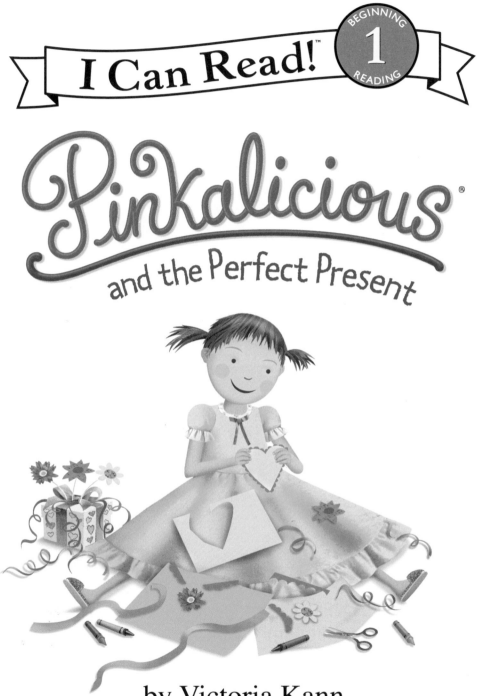

Pinkalicious®
and the Perfect Present

by Victoria Kann

HARPER

An Imprint of HarperCollinsPublishers

Mommy and I were riding our bike

when I saw something ahead

that looked like it might be fun.

"Look, Mommy," I said.

"There's a yard sale!

You might find a vase!

I might find some pretty jewelry!

Let's go find some treasures!"

Mommy smiled.

"Maybe I'll find a book

for us to read together," she said.

"Here are two dollars to buy
yourself a present," said Mommy.
"I'm Sally," said the yard sale lady.
"Let me know if you need any help."

Then I saw my friend Molly.

"Hi, Pinkalicious!" Molly called.

"Where do you think
I can find some fish?"

Next I saw my friend, Lila!

She had on a dress, a necklace,

a hat, and big sunglasses.

They were all purple!

12

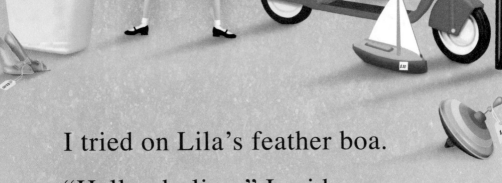

I tried on Lila's feather boa.

"Hello, darling," I said.

"Don't you just love the opera?"

Molly found some fishing treasures.

Lila found dress-up treasures.

I hadn't found anything interesting.

If I was ever going to find

my own treasure,

I needed a plan.

"I know," I said. "I'll look for pink!"

All of a sudden,

I saw pink everywhere.

Now I had lots to choose from.

I could hardly carry it all!

"You need this pink wagon
to carry your collection!" said Sally.

"This hat is perfectly pinkerrific,"
I said, and twisted to my left.

"This tea set would be pinkatastic
for a party," I said,
and twirled to my right.

"Whoops! Now I'm dizzy!"

"Wow, look at that!" I gasped.

I saw something that

was better than all the rest.

It was pinkaperfect!

It was a pinkatastic music box!
"I know this song," I said.
"Mommy sings it to me
at bedtime."

I had found something amazing.

I had finally found a treasure.

I didn't want the tea set.

I didn't want the hat.

I wanted the music box,

but not for me.

"How much is this?" I asked.

"Two dollars," said Sally.

It would be a surprise for Mommy.

Then I thought of a problem.

"Uh-oh," I said.

I whispered in Sally's ear.

"Hmmm. Let me think," said Sally.

"I've got it!" Sally said.

"Take this old purse for free
and hide the gift inside!"

"Mommy will think I got the purse
and won't see the present.

Thanks, Sally!" I said.

The next morning I got up early.

I made a card that said

I LOVE YOU.

I wrapped the present.

Mommy came in with her coffee.

I hid behind the sofa.

"What is this?" Mommy asked.

She had unwrapped my present

and was holding up the music box.

29

I jumped out and yelled, "Surprise!

Look what I got for you!

It's a music box.

Listen . . ."

I turned the key.

"Oh my, it's my favorite song!"
Mommy said.

"I told you we'd find a treasure
at the yard sale!" I said.

Mommy gave me a hug.

Sometimes the best presents

are the ones you give!